W9-APA-867

LIGHTHOUSE FAMILY

THE TURTLE

BY CYNTHIA RYLANT

ILLUSTRATED BY PRESTON McDANIELS

ALADDIN PAPERBACKS

New York   London   Toronto   Sydney

For D, who found the lights—C. R.

For Bruce T.—P. McD.

ALADDIN PAPERBACKS
An imprint of Simon & Schuster Children's Publishing Division
1230 Avenue of the Americas, New York, NY 10020
Text copyright © 2005 by Cynthia Rylant
Illustrations copyright © 2005 by Preston McDaniels
All rights reserved, including the right of reproduction in whole or in part in any form.
ALADDIN PAPERBACKS and colophon are trademarks of
Simon & Schuster, Inc.
Also available in a Simon & Schuster Books for Young Readers hardcover edition.
The text of this book was set in Centaur.
The illustrations for this book were rendered in graphite.
Manufactured in the United States of America
First Aladdin Paperbacks edition February 2006
2 4 6 8 10 9 7 5 3 1
The Library of Congress has cataloged the hardcover edition as follows:
Rylant, Cynthia.
The lighthouse family. The turtle / Cynthia Rylant ;
illustrated by Preston McDaniels.—1st ed.
p. cm.
title: Turtle.
Summary: When Aurora the sea turtle becomes stranded in fog and
cold water near a lighthouse, Pandora the cat, Seabold the dog,
and their three adopted mouse children call on the pelicans for help.
ISBN-13: 978-0-689-86244-1 (hc.)
ISBN-10: 0-689-86244-X (hc.)
[1. Animals—Fiction. 2. Sea turtles—Fiction. 3. Turtles—Fiction.
4. Pelicans—Fiction. 5. Auroras—Fiction. 6. Lighthouses—Fiction.] I. Title: Turtle.
II. McDaniels, Preston, ill. III. Title.
PZ7.R982Lge 2005
[E]—dc22 2004007447
ISBN-13: 978-0-689-86312-7 (Aladdin pbk.)
ISBN-10: 0-689-86312-8 (Aladdin pbk.)

Contents

1. *Fog*

At the edge of a rocky cliff, high above the beautiful waves of a blue-green sea, there stood a proud lighthouse, and in this lighthouse there lived a family.

This was an unusual family, but a very happy one. At one time they had all been scattered about the world, living very different lives, never knowing that the future would one day bring them together.

There was Pandora, the cat, who had lived all alone at the lighthouse. Bravely she tended the great lamp year after year to help those who sailed the seas in fog and darkness and who might be in danger of shipwreck. Seeing the bright beacon across the water, sailors carefully turned their ships away from the deadly rocks of the shore.

Seabold, the dog, was for many years a sailor himself and a very fine one. He was quite proud of the boat he called *Adventure*. But one dark night Seabold was tossed into the ocean in a storm, and though this might have been an unlucky turn in the dog's life, it was, in fact, good fortune. For Seabold washed up, alive, on Pandora's shore. Pandora found him, sheltered him, and they found in each other a true friend.

The dog, however, knew that he must return to the sea, to a sailor's life, once he and his boat were mended. Pandora knew this too, for the sea was the very heart of Seabold's life, and she understood.

But then one day they found the children, and everything changed.

Pandora spotted three orphan mice—Whistler, Lila, and their baby sister Tiny—adrift in a crate in the vast blue waters. The children, who had fled an uncertain fate in an orphanage, were carried into the lighthouse, warmed, fed, and, ultimately, loved.

Seabold did not leave. The children did not leave. Having found one another, everyone wanted to stay. So in the sanctuary that was Pandora's lonely lighthouse, they all became a family. And the lighthouse was lonely no more.

Now winter was nearing. The days were shorter and colder, and a thick, damp fog rolled into shore nearly every morning. From their cottage window high on the cliff, Whistler and Lila could see the clear blue sky above them but only a gray cotton blanket of fog below. Sometimes they saw the masts of small boats poking up through the fog like twigs in a snowdrift.

Lighthouse keeping became very important work in these times. Seabold often stood at the edge of the cliff for hours, sounding a foghorn in his hands, guiding small boats in to shore and warning the large schooners away. Lila and Whistler loved to be near Seabold as he worked, but on the windiest days Pandora so worried they might be blown off the cliff that she insisted the children tie themselves

to the porch post. This, of course, required the children to be very creative in their play. They also had to be patient, for they could hear each other's voices only between the blasts of Seabold's horn.

"Let's pretend we've been captured by pirates," suggested Whistler. "They've tied us to the masts until we tell them where the treasure is."

"Let's be kites," said Lila, spreading her arms wide and spinning in circles.

Seabold sounded the horn. The children waited.

When all was quiet again, Whistler said, *"Brrrr.* It's so cold today. Maybe we should just pretend we're on our way home for tea."

"Yes!" said Lila, shivering and tucking in her scarf. "Let's pretend we live right here and can run inside and get warm."

"And that someone nice will bake us something toasty," said Whistler.

"And sweet," added Lila.

She looked at her brother.

"Isn't it nice we don't have to pretend *that* story?" Lila asked with a smile.

But just as Whistler was about to answer, they suddenly heard a voice from the thick fog below:

"Hello? Hello up there?"

Lila looked at Whistler.

"Goodness," she said.

"Who is it, Seabold?" called Whistler.

"Did you hear?" called Lila. She wished she could untie herself and run to Seabold's side. But

she knew she must mind Pandora.

"Who goes there?" Seabold shouted down into the fog bank.

He waited for an answer. The children waited for an answer. None came.

Seabold returned to the children and gathered up the ropes, which had kept them safe.

"I am going down to the shore, children," Seabold said. "You must go inside and wait with Pandora. And have her set hot tea to brewing, for that was a very mysterious call. Who knows what I might bring back."

"May I come with you, Seabold?" asked Whistler.

"And I?" asked Lila.

Seabold carefully studied them.

"Please?" asked Whistler. "We like to help."

Seabold smiled and patted the boy's shoulder.

"Indeed you do," he said. "Run, then. Tell Pandora."

The children hurried into the kitchen to tell

Pandora the news. Pandora was mixing up something in a bowl while Tiny slept tucked in a candlesnuffer on the windowsill.

"Oh, yes," said Pandora. "Do go. Seabold may need your help."

She lifted up the ends of the ropes still attached to the children.

"But see to it that you are safely tied to Seabold," she said. "A strong gust and I dread to think what might happen."

The children ran back outside. Then, with the ends of their safety ropes looped to the buttons of Seabold's coat, they started carefully down the cliff to see who might be helped.

2. The Turtle

The steep sides of the cliff were very slippery. As the children made their way down to the shore they were very glad indeed they were anchored to Seabold, for they could barely hold their footing. As they descended the fog became thicker and thicker.

When they reached the bottom, Lila took Seabold's paw.

"Where are we, Seabold?" asked Lila, reaching out into the eerie whiteness.

"Why, we are just below the lighthouse, child," said Seabold.

"How will we find our way back?" asked Lila. "I can't see even my feet."

Seabold chuckled.

"You forget what a fine nose I have," said the dog. "Don't worry. I can smell the crackling wood of our kitchen stove from here.

"Now, children," said Seabold, "let's be quiet and listen."

The three stood silently, straining to hear anyone who might be lost in the dense mist.

"Hello?" called a voice. *"Hello?"*

"HELLO!" boomed Seabold. "WE ARE HERE!"

Seabold guided the children carefully to the east.

"WE ARE COMING!" shouted Seabold.

"I'm here!" answered the voice. *"I'm here!"*

With the help of Seabold's strong voice and fine nose, he and the children made their slow way to the lost voice in the fog.

As they came nearer the *hellos* and *right here*s being called, Whistler spotted a smooth large rock up ahead.

"I think whoever it is is behind that rock!" he said.

They all stepped carefully toward it.

Suddenly the rock lifted its head.

Whistler, Lila—even Seabold—jumped in surprise!

The rock said, "I am so happy to see you."

"Heavens!" said Whistler. "It's a sea turtle!"

Seabold crouched down. The children stepped in closer. And everyone looked into a gentle green face and round eyes flowing with tears.

"My name is Aurora," said the turtle.

"Oh, dear," said Lila, reaching into her pocket. "You need a hankie."

The turtle smiled.

"No, it's all right," said Aurora. "Sea turtles often cry. But we aren't sad."

Seabold tipped his hat.

"I am Seabold," he said, "and this is Whistler and his sister Lila. We keep the lighthouse on the hill, and we've come to help you."

"Oh, thank you, thank you," said Aurora. "I heard your horn. I was hurrying south when a gale caught me and blew me into this fog. And now I am so very cold. I shouldn't be here at all, really. Sea turtles are not made for these northern waters."

"Why did you swim north?" asked Whistler.

"That story can wait, I think," said Seabold. "First we must find a way to help Aurora keep warm."

"We have a nice stove in the lighthouse," said Lila.

Seabold looked above him and sighed.

"Yes, but that cliff is much too difficult a climb for Aurora," he said.

More tears fell from Aurora's eyes.

"Are those sad tears now?" asked Lila.

Aurora nodded her head.

"Oh dear," said Lila.

"Pandora is our problem solver," said Seabold. "She will know what to do."

"But we can't leave Aurora here alone," said Whistler.

"Exactly," said Seabold. "And that is why you and Lila will be staying here with her until I return with Pandora."

"Yes!" Lila. "Good idea."

Seabold pulled off his coat and draped it across Aurora's back.

"This will help keep you warm," he said. "And the children are nicely attached to it, so no one will stray in the fog. I'll be back quickly and everything will be just fine."

Whistler looked at Aurora.

"It always is," he said, "with Seabold and Pandora."

"Would you like a hankie now?" asked Lila.

Aurora smiled.

"Yes," she said, sniffling. "Thank you."

3. The Plan

While Seabold was away fetching Pandora, the children learned why Aurora had traveled so far north.

"I wanted to see the northern lights," said Aurora.

"The northern lights?" asked Whistler.

"Yes," said Aurora. "In fact, I was named for them. *Aurora borealis.* Someone told my mother about the lights when she was small, and she dreamed of seeing them one day. But we sea turtles are meant to stay in warm waters, and she was afraid to venture north."

Aurora smiled proudly.

"Instead, she named her first baby Aurora.

And all my long life I have promised myself to see the lights for which I was named."

"And did you see them?" asked Lila.

"Oh, yes," said Aurora. "Yes, I did."

"What did they look like?" asked Whistler.

Aurora looked at the children, her large gentle eyes full of tears.

"They were more beautiful than any sunrise or sunset that I have ever seen. More beautiful than the moon and stars. More beautiful than a coral reef."

"Really?" asked Lila.

Aurora nodded.

"The lights filled up the black sky with pinks and blues and greens, and they moved like water. They rippled and flowed like water. But they were lights."

"I would give anything to see that," said Whistler.

"Though it took me a hundred years, I found them," said Aurora. "You will surely find them too someday."

"A hundred years?" repeated Lila.

"Since the day I was born," answered Aurora.

"Goodness," said Lila. "You've seen many things."

"Yes," said Aurora. "But nothing so beautiful as the northern lights."

"Are you still cold?" asked Whistler. "Maybe you should pull inside your shell for warmth."

"Sea turtles cannot tuck inside their shells like land turtles do," said Aurora. "We must face what comes our way."

"Well, soon *help* will come your way," said Lila.

"HELLO!" called Seabold's voice from the fog.

"See?" said Lila to Aurora.

"*Over here, Seabold!*" shouted Whistler.

"Carefully, carefully. Watch your step," came Seabold's patient voice through the fog. Then there they were, Seabold and Pandora, carrying buckets, come to help.

"Pandora, this is our friend Aurora," said Whistler.

Pandora set down her bucket and smiled at the turtle.

"I'm so pleased to meet you, Aurora," she said. "And so sorry for your distress."

"Thank you," said Aurora. "But I think I am actually *happy* being here. I am making wonderful friends."

Seabold smiled and pointed to his wool cap.

"And here is another. We brought along Tiny."

Aurora looked up at the small baby mouse, wrapped snugly in the roll of Seabold's cap, wearing a tiny sock on her head.

"Oh," said Aurora, "a beautiful baby."

"We must warm you up," said Pandora. "I have a plan to get you home, but first we must warm you up."

She knelt down and removed the lid from her

bucket. She lifted out a smooth rock with her mittened paws.

"Seabold and I heated these stones in the stove," said Pandora. "They will keep their heat through the morning, then we will bring more."

Pandora turned to Whistler and Lila.

"Children, can you place these all around Aurora's shell, to keep her warm?"

"Certainly!" said Whistler.

As the children carefully encircled Aurora's shell with the toasty stones, Pandora pulled from her pockets hot acorn muffins wrapped in warm towels and a jar of canned beets.

"I thought you might be hungry," said Pandora.

"Oh, yes," said Aurora. "Thank you very much."

As everyone shared the muffins and beets and the warmth of the heated stones, Pandora began to speak of her plan.

"The pelicans will be passing through any day now," said Pandora. "I checked my logbook, and they are due on their journey south.

"I know many of the pelicans by name," Pandora continued, "for they sometimes rest on the roof of the lighthouse. And I have even mended a few wings, a favor I know they would love to repay."

Pandora looked at the children. She looked at Aurora. She smiled.

"Now, this is my plan," she said.

They all listened closely to Pandora's plan. And when she had finished, everyone had the same reaction: *"Brilliant!"*

4. The Pelicans

During the next few days, Whistler and Lila made many trips down to the shore to tend to Aurora. Pandora and Seabold needed to take care of both the lighthouse and Tiny, so the two children had the important duty of helping the turtle. They brought her warm food wrapped up in their twine bags, including baked wild potatoes ("astonishing," said Aurora) and stir-fried nettles ("heavenly," she said). The children told her their stories and she listened to them. And all were made happy when Seabold arrived with more hot stones.

Finally, on the third morning of waiting, a lone pelican flew across the water. The children were having breakfast with Pandora and Seabold in the kitchen when Lila spotted the bird.

"A pelican! They're coming!" she cried.

Everyone ran outside. Off in the distance they could see at least a dozen of the large birds flying in the direction of the lighthouse.

"Flutter your aprons, children! Flutter your aprons!" said Pandora. She had given everybody one of her aprons to wave, to signal the pelicans to land.

"I hope they don't think I wear this," said Seabold, fluttering the apron in his paw.

"Nor I," said Whistler.

One by one the pelicans began to land. When they were finished, there were fifteen in all.

"Greetings, Pandora," said one of the birds. He stretched his giant pouch so wide that Lila nervously backed away.

"Hello, Augustus," said Pandora. "So nice to see you again. Did you have a good summer at the pole?"

"Perfect," said the pelican.

"Oh, good," said Pandora. "I need your help,

Augustus. First let me introduce my family, then I'll explain."

Pandora introduced the children and Seabold to Augustus and all of the other pelicans.

"Pandora, I am glad you have this little family now," said Augustus. "I see contentment in you."

"Thank you, Augustus," said Pandora.

"Now, how may I help you?" asked the bird.

Pandora explained the situation. She told the pelicans how Aurora had become stranded in a fog and was unable to complete her journey south, for the waters were now much too cold. The turtle needed to go home, yet she could not swim.

"But how does one travel the ocean if not by swimming?" asked Augustus.

Pandora looked at him and quietly answered. "Why, by flying, of course."

And within a very short time, a one-hundred-year-old sea turtle found herself surrounded by six strong pelicans, sailing rope stretching from their beaks and wrapping around her shell like the handles of a fishnet bag.

"You mustn't worry," Pandora said softly to Aurora. "Pelicans have the longest wings of most birds I know. Their wings are like the sails of the tallest ships, and when the wind catches them, the birds will fly. And so will you."

"You'll be home tomorrow," said Seabold, "by my calculations."

Aurora looked bravely at them both, and at Whistler and Lila who stood by their sides, and at baby Tiny in the roll of Seabold's cap.

"I'm not afraid," said Aurora. "I have seen the northern lights."

Lila pulled something from the pocket of her dress.

"Whistler and I made this for you, Aurora, to remember us by," said Lila.

She lifted the turtle's front flipper and slid a shell bracelet onto it. The largest shell, in the middle, glowed with pinks and blues and greens.

"That's an abalone shell I found after a storm," said Whistler. "It has the colors of the aurora borealis."

Big round tears dropped from the sea turtle's eyes.

"Oh dear," said Lila, pulling out her hankie.

"I will never forget you," said Aurora. "Any of you.

"*Bon voyage*, Aurora," said Seabold.

"Godspeed," said Pandora.

And with a word from Augustus, the six strong pelicans spread their long, long wings, caught the wind, and lifted the turtle into the air.

"Good-bye! Good-bye!" called the lighthouse family.

"Good-bye!" called Aurora.

And the family watched in silence as the sea turtle disappeared into the blue horizon.

Lila's wide eyes were wet.

"Oh, dear," said Pandora, pulling out a hankie.

"Well done," said Seabold, patting Whistler on the shoulder. "Well done."

On the way back to the lighthouse, Whistler asked Seabold if they might sail north to see the lights one day.

And the dog answered, "Absolutely. Oh yes, absolutely."